HORRiD HENRY'S
Birthday Party

HORRID HENRY'S
Birthday Party

Francesca Simon
Illustrated by Tony Ross

Orion
Children's Books

Horrid Henry's Birthday Party originally appeared in
Horrid Henry and the Secret Club first published in Great Britain in 1995
by Orion Children's Books
This edition first published in Great Britain in 2009
by Orion Children's Books
a division of the Orion Publishing Group Ltd
Orion House
5 Upper Saint Martin's Lane
London WC2H 9EA
An Hachette Livre UK Company

1 3 5 7 9 8 6 4 2

Text © Francesca Simon 1995
Illustrations © Tony Ross 2009

The Orion Publishing Group's policy is to use papers that
are natural, renewable and recyclable products and made
from wood grown in sustainable forests. The logging and
manufacturing processes are expected to conform to the
environmental regulations of the country of origin.

A catalogue record for this book is available from the British Library.

ISBN 978 1 84255 722 8

Printed by Printer Trento, Italy

www.orionbooks.co.uk
www.horridhenry.co.uk

To my agent, Rosemary Sandberg,
with grateful thanks

Contents

Chapter 1

February was Horrid Henry's
favourite month.
His birthday was in February.

"It's my birthday soon!" said Henry
every day after Christmas.

"And my birthday party! Hurray!"

February was Horrid Henry's parents' least favourite month.

"It's Henry's birthday soon," said Dad, groaning.

"And his birthday party," said Mum, groaning even louder.

Every year they thought Henry's
birthday parties could not get worse.
But they always did.

Every year Henry's parents said they
would never ever let Henry have
a birthday party again.
But every year they gave Henry
one absolutely last final chance.

Henry had big plans for this
year's party.

"I want to go to Lazer Zap,"
said Henry. He'd been to Lazer Zap
for Tough Toby's party. They'd had a
great time dressing up as spacemen
and blasting each other in dark
tunnels all afternoon.

"NO!" said Mum. "Too violent."
"I agree," said Dad.
"And too expensive," said Mum.
"I agree," said Dad.

There was a moment's silence.

"However," said Dad, "it does mean
the party wouldn't be here."

Mum looked at Dad.
Dad looked at Mum.
"How do I book?" said Mum.

"Hurray!" shrieked Henry.

ZAP!
ZAP! ZAP!
ZAP!

Chapter 2

Horrid Henry sat in his fort holding a pad of paper. On the front cover in big capital letters Henry wrote:

HENRY'S
PARTY PLANS

TOP SECRET!!!!

At the top of the first page Henry had written:

Guests

A long list followed.
Then Henry stared at the names
and chewed his pencil.

Actually, I don't
want Margaret,
thought Henry.
Too moody.
He crossed out
Moody Margaret's
name.

Margaret

And I definitely
don't want Susan.
Too crabby.

Susan

In fact, I don't want any girls at all,
thought Henry.

He crossed out
Clever Clare

Clare

and Lazy Linda.   Linda

Then there was Anxious Andrew.

Nope, thought
Henry, crossing
him off.
He's no fun.

Andrew

Toby

Toby was
possible, but
Henry didn't
really like him.
Out went
Tough Toby.

William?
No way, thought
Henry. He'll be
crying the second
he gets zapped.
Out went Weepy
William.

william

Ralph?
Henry considered.
Ralph would be
good because he was
sure to get into trouble.
On the other hand,
he hadn't invited Henry to *his* party.

Ralph

Rude Ralph was struck off.

So were
Babbling Bob,
Jolly Josh,

Bob

Josh

Greedy Graham
and Dizzy Dave.

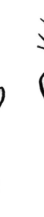

Graham

Dave

24

And absolutely no way was
Peter coming anywhere near him
on his birthday.

Peter

Ahh, that was better. No horrid kids
would be coming to *his* party.

There was only one problem.
Every single name was crossed off.
No guests meant no presents.

Henry looked at his list. Margaret
was a moody old grouch and he
hated her, but she did sometimes
give good gifts. He still had the
jumbo box of day-glo slime she'd
given him last year.

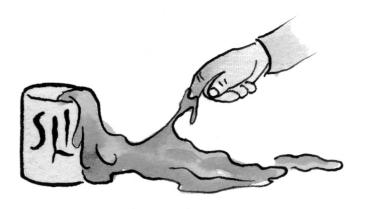

And Toby *had* invited Henry
to *his* party.

And Dave was always spinning round
like a top, falling and knocking things
over which was fun. Graham would
eat too much and burp.

And Ralph was sure to say
rude words and make all the
grown-ups angry.

Oh, let them all come,
thought Henry. Except Peter,
of course. The more guests I have,
the more presents I get!

Henry turned to the next page
and wrote:

PRESENTS I WANT

Super Soaker 2000,
the best water blaster ever

Spy Fax

Micro Machines

Slime

Nintendo

Inter-galactic Samurai Gorillas

Stink bombs

Pet rats

Whoopee cushion

25-gear mountain bike

Money

He'd leave the list lying around where Mum and Dad were sure to find it.

Chapter 3

"I've done the menu for the party," said Mum. "What do you think?"

> ## MUM'S MENU
>
> carrot sticks
>
> cucumber sandwiches
>
> peanut butter sandwiches
>
> grapes
>
> raisins
>
> apple juice
>
> carrot cake

"**Blecccccch**," said Henry. "I don't want that horrible food at my party. I want food that I like."

Henry's Menu

Pickled Onion Monster Munch
Smoky Spider Shreddies
Super Spicy Hedgehog Crisps
Crunchy Crackles
Twizzle Fizzle Sticks
Purple Planet-buster Drink
chocolate bars
chocolate eggs
Chocolate Monster Cake

"You can't just have junk food,"
said Mum.
"It's not junk food," said Henry.
"Crisps are made from potatoes,
and Monster Munch has onions –
that's two vegetables."

"Henry . . ." said Mum.
She looked fierce.

Henry looked at his menu. Then he
added, in small letters at the bottom:

peanut butter sandwiches

"But only in the middle of the table," said Henry. "So no one has to eat them who doesn't want them."

"All right," said Mum.
Years of fighting with Henry about his parties had worn her down.

"And Peter's not coming,"
said Henry.

"What?!" said Perfect Peter, looking
up from polishing his shoes.

"Peter is your brother. Of course
he's invited."

Henry
scowled.
"But he'll ruin
everything."

"No Peter, no party," said Mum.

Henry pretended he was a fire-breathing dragon.

"**Owww!**" shrieked Peter.

Don't be horrid, Henry!

"All right,"
said Henry.
"He can come. But you'd better keep
out of my way," he hissed at Peter.

"Mum!" wailed Peter.
"Henry's being mean to me."

"Stop it, Henry," said Mum.

Henry decided to change the
subject fast. "What about party bags?"
said Henry.

"I want everyone to have Slime, and loads and loads and loads of sweets! Dirt Balls, Nose Pickers and Foam Teeth are the best."

"We'll see," said Mum. She looked at the calendar. Only two more days. Soon it would be over.

Chapter 4

Henry's birthday arrived at last.

"Happy birthday, Henry!" said Peter.
"Where are my presents?"
said Henry.

Dad pointed. Horrid Henry
attacked the pile.

Mum and Dad
had given him
a First
Encyclopaedia,
Scrabble,
a fountain pen,
a hand-knitted
cardigan,
a globe, and
three sets of
vests and pants.

"Oh," said Henry. He pushed the
dreadful presents aside.

"Anything else?" he asked hopefully.
Maybe they were keeping the
Super Soaker for last.
"I've got a present for you," said
Peter. "I chose it myself."
Henry tore off the wrapping paper.
It was a tapestry kit.

"Yuck!"

"I'll have it if you don't want it,"
said Peter.
"No!" said Henry, snatching
up the kit.

"Wasn't it a great idea to have Henry's party at Lazer Zap?" said Dad.
"Yes," said Mum. "No mess, no fuss."
They smiled at each other.

Ring   ring.

Dad answered the phone.
It was the Lazer Zap lady.
"Hello! I was just ringing to check the birthday boy's name," she said.
"We like to announce it over our loudspeaker during the party."

Dad gave Henry's name.
A terrible scream came from the
other end of the phone. Dad held
the receiver away from his ear.

The shrieking and screaming
continued.

"Hmmmn," said Dad. "I see. Thank
you." Dad hung up. He looked pale.

Henry!

Yeah?

"Is it true that you wrecked the place when you went to Lazer Zap with Toby?" said Dad.
"No!" said Henry.
He tried to look harmless.
"And trampled on several children?"

"No!" said Henry.
"Yes you did," said Perfect Peter.

"And what about all the lasers you broke?"

"What lasers?" said Henry.

"And the slime you put in the space suits?" said Peter.

"That wasn't me, telltale," shrieked Henry. "What about my party?"

45

"I'm afraid Lazer Zap
have banned you," said Dad.

"But what about Henry's party?"
said Mum. She looked pale.

"But what about my party?!" wailed
Henry. "I want to go to Lazer Zap!"

"Never mind," said Dad brightly.
"I know lots of good games."

Chapter 5

Ding dong.

It was the first guest, Sour Susan.
She held a large present.
Henry snatched the package.

It was a pad of paper and
some felt tip pens.
"How lovely," said Mum.
"What do you say, Henry?"
"I've already got that," said Henry.

Don't be
horrid, Henry!

I don't care, thought Henry.
This was the worst day of his life.

Ding dong.

It was the second guest, Anxious
Andrew. He held a tiny present.
Henry snatched the package.
"It's awfully small," said Henry, tearing
off the wrapping. "And it smells."

It was a box of animal soaps.

"How super," said Dad.
"What do you say, Henry?"

Ugghhh!

Don't be horrid, Henry!

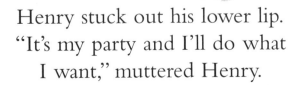

Henry stuck out his lower lip.
"It's my party and I'll do what
I want," muttered Henry.

"Watch your step, young man,"
said Dad.
Henry stuck out his tongue
behind Dad's back.

More guests arrived.

Lazy Linda gave him a "Read and Listen" CD of favourite fairy tales: Cinderella, Snow White, and Sleeping Beauty.

"Fabulous," said Mum.

"Yuck!"

said Henry.

Clever Clare handed him
a square package.

Henry held it by the corners.
"It's a book," he groaned.

"My favourite present!" said Peter.
"Wonderful," said Mum.
"What is it?"
Henry unwrapped it slowly.

"Great!" said Perfect Peter.
"Can I borrow it?"

"NO!" screamed Henry.
Then he threw the book on the floor
and stomped on it.

"Henry!" hissed Mum. "I'm warning
you. When someone gives you a
present you say thank you."

Rude Ralph was the last to arrive. He handed Henry a long rectangular package wrapped in newspaper.

It was a Super Soaker 2000 water blaster.

"Oh,"
said Mum.

"Put it away,"
said Dad.

"Thank you, Ralph," beamed Henry.
"Just what I wanted."

Chapter 6

"Let's start with Pass the Parcel,"
said Dad.
"I hate Pass the Parcel,"
said Horrid Henry.
What a horrible party this was.

"I love Pass the Parcel," said
Perfect Peter.

"I don't want
to play," said
Sour Susan.

"When do
we eat?" said
Greedy Graham.

Dad started the music.
"Pass the parcel, William," said Dad.

"No!"

shrieked William. "It's mine!"
"But the music is still playing,"
said Dad.
William burst into tears.
Horrid Henry tried to snatch
the parcel.

Dad stopped the music.

William stopped crying instantly
and tore off the wrapping.
"A granola bar," he said.

"That's a
terrible
prize," said
Rude Ralph.

"Is it my turn yet?"
said Anxious Andrew.

"When do we eat?"
said Greedy Graham.

"I hate Pass the Parcel,"
screamed Henry.
"I want to play
something else."

"Musical Statues!"
announced Mum brightly.

"You're out, Henry,"
said Dad.
"You moved."

"I didn't," said Henry.

"Yes you did," said Toby.

"No, I didn't," said Henry.
"I'm not leaving."

"That's not fair,"
shrieked Sour Susan.

"I'm not
playing," whined
Dizzy Dave.

"I'm tired," sulked Lazy Linda.

"I hate Musical Statues," moaned Moody Margaret.

"Where's my prize?" demanded
Rude Ralph.
"A bookmark?" said Ralph.
"That's it?"

"Tea time!" said Dad.

The children pushed and shoved
their way to the table, grabbing and
snatching at the food.

"I hate fizzy drinks,"
said Tough Toby.

"I feel sick," said Greedy Graham.

"Where are the carrot sticks?"
said Perfect Peter.

Horrid Henry sat at the head
of the table. He didn't feel like
throwing food at Clare.
He didn't feel like rampaging with
Toby and Ralph. He didn't even feel
like kicking Peter.
He wanted to be at Lazer Zap.

Then Henry had a wonderful,
spectacular idea. He got up and
sneaked out of the room.

"Party bags," said Dad.

"What's in them?" said Tough Toby.
"Seedlings," said Mum.
"Where are the sweets?"
said Greedy Graham.
"This is the worst party bag
I've ever had," said Rude Ralph.

There was a noise outside.
Then Henry burst into the kitchen,
Super Soaker in hand.

shrieked Henry, drenching everyone
with water. "Ha! Ha! Gotcha!"

Splat went the cake.

Splash went the drinks.

"EEEEEEEEEEEEEEKKK!"

shrieked the sopping wet children.

"HENRY!!!!"
yelled Mum
and Dad.

"YOU HORRID BOY!"
yelled Mum.
Water dripped from her hair.
"GO TO YOUR ROOM!"

"THIS IS YOUR LAST
PARTY EVER!" yelled Dad.
Water dripped from his clothes.

But Henry didn't care.
They said that every year.

More
HORRiD HENRY

For younger readers
Don't Be Horrid, Henry
More titles coming soon . . .

HORRiD HENRY Books
Horrid Henry
Horrid Henry and the Secret Club
Horrid Henry Tricks the Tooth Fairy
Horrid Henry's Nits
Horrid Henry Gets Rich Quick
Horrid Henry's Haunted House
Horrid Henry and the Mummy's Curse
Horrid Henry's Revenge
Horrid Henry and the Bogey Babysitter
Horrid Henry's Stinkbomb
Horrid Henry's Underpants
Horrid Henry Meets the Queen
Horrid Henry and the Mega-Mean Time Machine
Horrid Henry and the Football Fiend
Horrid Henry's Christmas Cracker

Horrid Henry and the Abominable Snowman
Horrid Henry Robs the Bank

Colour books
Horrid Henry's Big Bad Book
Horrid Henry's Wicked Ways
Horrid Henry's Evil Enemies
Horrid Henry Rules the World
Horrid Henry's House of Horrors

Joke Books
Horrid Henry's Joke Book
Horrid Henry's Jolly Joke Book
Horrid Henry's Mighty Joke Book

Activity Books
Horrid Henry's Brainbusters
Horrid Henry's Headscratchers
Horrid Henry's Mindbenders
Horrid Henry's Colouring Book
Horrid Henry's Puzzle Book
Horrid Henry's Sticker Book
Horrid Henry's Mad Mazes
Horrid Henry's Wicked Wordsearches
Horrid Henry's Crazy Crosswords